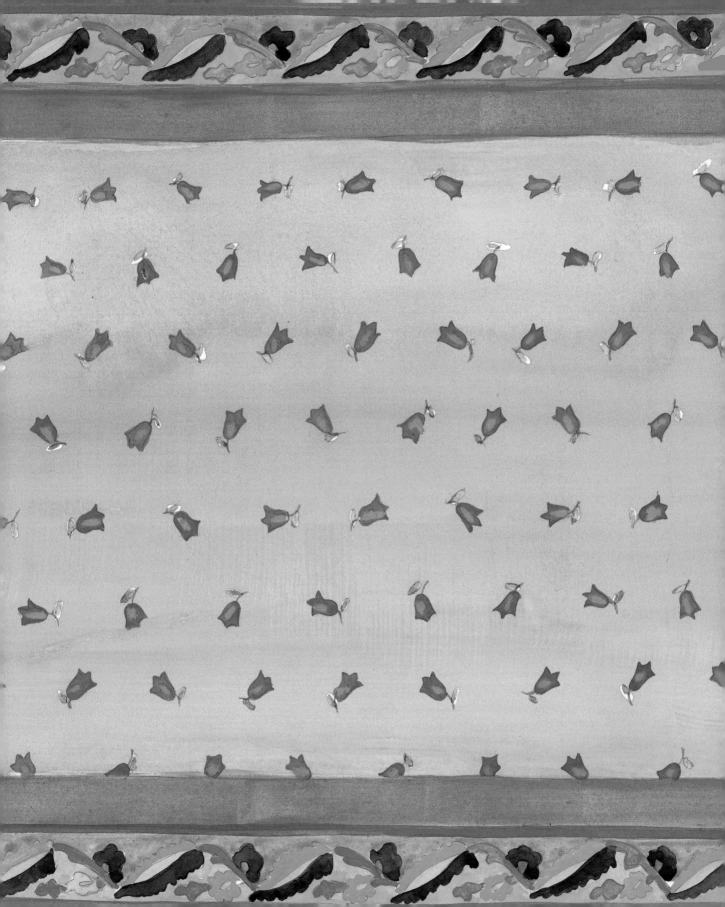

Gigi & Jacques' Picnic in Provence

written & illustrated by
Maureen Edgecomb

PUBLISHED EXCLUSIVELY

for

Published in the United States 2004
by Ravenwood Studios
P.O. Box 197
Diamond Springs, California 95619

Exclusively for
Caesars Entertainment Corporation

Gigi Paris and Jacques are trademarks of Caesars Entertainment Corporation

Book Design by Ruth Marcus, Sequim, WA

Printed in China

First Edition

ISBN # 0-9718604-4-0

Gigi and Jacques loved to take walks through Paris
and talk about everything.
They talked and barked and woofed and talked.

"We're different, aren't we, Gigi?"
Jacques asked.

"Why, yes, Jacques. I'm a poodle
and you're a bulldog."

"Oui," Jacques replied, "and I like
bones, and you like biscuits.
But we can be different and still
be friends and still see each other
every day. Except tomorrow."

"Tomorrow?" Gigi asked.
"Oui. Philippe said we are taking a break to go away to the country to paint."

"Oh, dear," Gigi sighed. "Maybe that's why Claudette is planning a trip to buy fabric."

"How long is a break?" Gigi asked.
Jacques looked puzzled.
"I don't know," he said.
"You don't know? Maybe it could be forever!"

"F-O-R-E-V-E-R-?"

Jacques pleaded with Philippe. "No, Philippe, please understand.
I don't want to go!" Jacques begged.
But Philippe had made up his mind. They were going.
Claudette said, "Allons, Gigi. We must go. We have to pack for our trip."

"It's just for a little while, Gigi.
We'll see beautiful fabrics and lots of flowers.
You'll see." But Gigi only wanted to see Jacques.

"It's only for a little while, Jacques.
We'll see beautiful hillsides and clouds to paint.
You can run and play in the fields. You'll see."
But Jacques only wanted to see Gigi.

Jacques and Philippe went on a train.

Gigi and Claudette went on a train, too.

But Jacques only wanted to be in Paris with his Gigi.

And Gigi could only think of Jacques.

When their train first stopped at Versailles,
Gigi and Jacques each visited the Hall of Mirrors.
But everywhere they looked, they could only see each other.
"Oh, I miss Jacques," Gigi sighed.

"I miss Gigi so much, all I see is Gigi everywhere!"
And soon they were back on the train to Provence.
And no one—not Jacques, Gigi, Philippe or Claudette—
knew they were all on the same train since they left Paris!

After they arrived in Provence,
Claudette shopped . . .

. . . and shopped . . .

. . . and shopped . . .

Philippe painted . . .

. . . and painted . . .

. . . and painted . . .

Finally, Claudette found what she was looking for.
"Gigi, look at this beautiful fabric!" She remarked.

Philippe then found the inspiration he was looking for.
Jacques didn't know he had stepped through some paint and
then on a canvas. Philippe saw his colorful prints and exclaimed,
"Jacques! Très magnifique! You are a true artist!"

Gigi and Claudette had just finished their shopping and were walking along a quaint little street when Gigi spotted colorful footprints.

She thought to hersel "That's something my Jacques would do."

"JACQUES!"
She barked out loud!

She pulled on her leash as tightly as she could to take Claudette around the corner.

And there they were! Philippe and Jacques were walking just ahead!

Whipping his head around, Jacques thought he was imagining Gigi's voice. But there she was!

He pulled Philippe around, and the four of them reunited right there on a street in Provence!

"Let's go on a picnic before we go home," Claudette said.

"What's a picnic?" Gigi asked Jacques.
Jacques explained, "You'll see, Gigi. It's great fun. Just like camping."
"Ladies don't go camping, Jacques."
"You'll see," he said. "It's great fun!"

So, they all strolled together through the shops of Provence and
gathered all they needed for a very special picnic.

They bought…

fruits and vegetables…and many other goodies, like…

…cheese…   …a blanket…   …pastry…

…bread…   …spring water…

…and most importantly…
…lots and lots of biscuits and bones.

They were all very happy to be together again.

At the picnic, Gigi and Jacques decided to explore the lavender field.

...and watch the clouds go by.

"Gigi," Jacques asked, "If you were a person, what would you be?"

"A model, a ballerina, a can-can girl, a fashion designer," she quickly answered

"What would you be, Jacques?"
He thought and thought and then answered,
"A sailor, a pirate, a waiter, a painter."

"But Jacques, I can't see you as any of those things.
I like you just the way you are."
Jacques was so happy, he rolled in the dirt!

As they started back to the picnic, all they could see was lavender everywhere they looked! Confused, Gigi barked, "Jacques, which way do we go?"

Their heads turned everywhere, but all they could see was lavender. "Je regrette, Gigi," Jacques answered, "I don't know!"

Just then, Gigi and Jacques heard Claudette calling, "Gigi, Jacques! It's time to catch the train!" So, they raced each other down the hill to Claudette and Philippe!

And they all took the romantic way home!

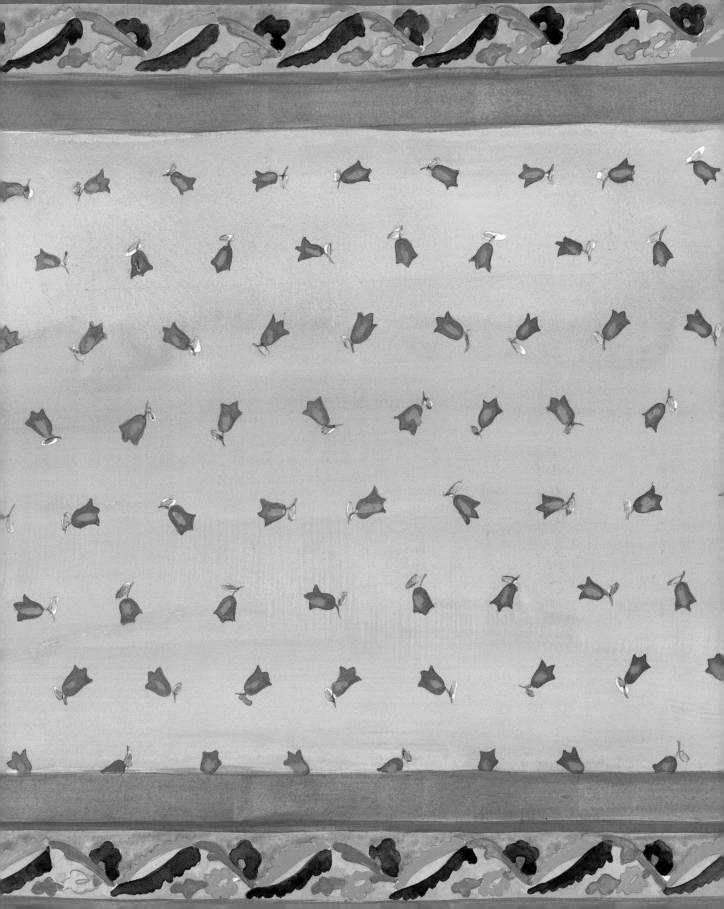